I love you
(nearly always)

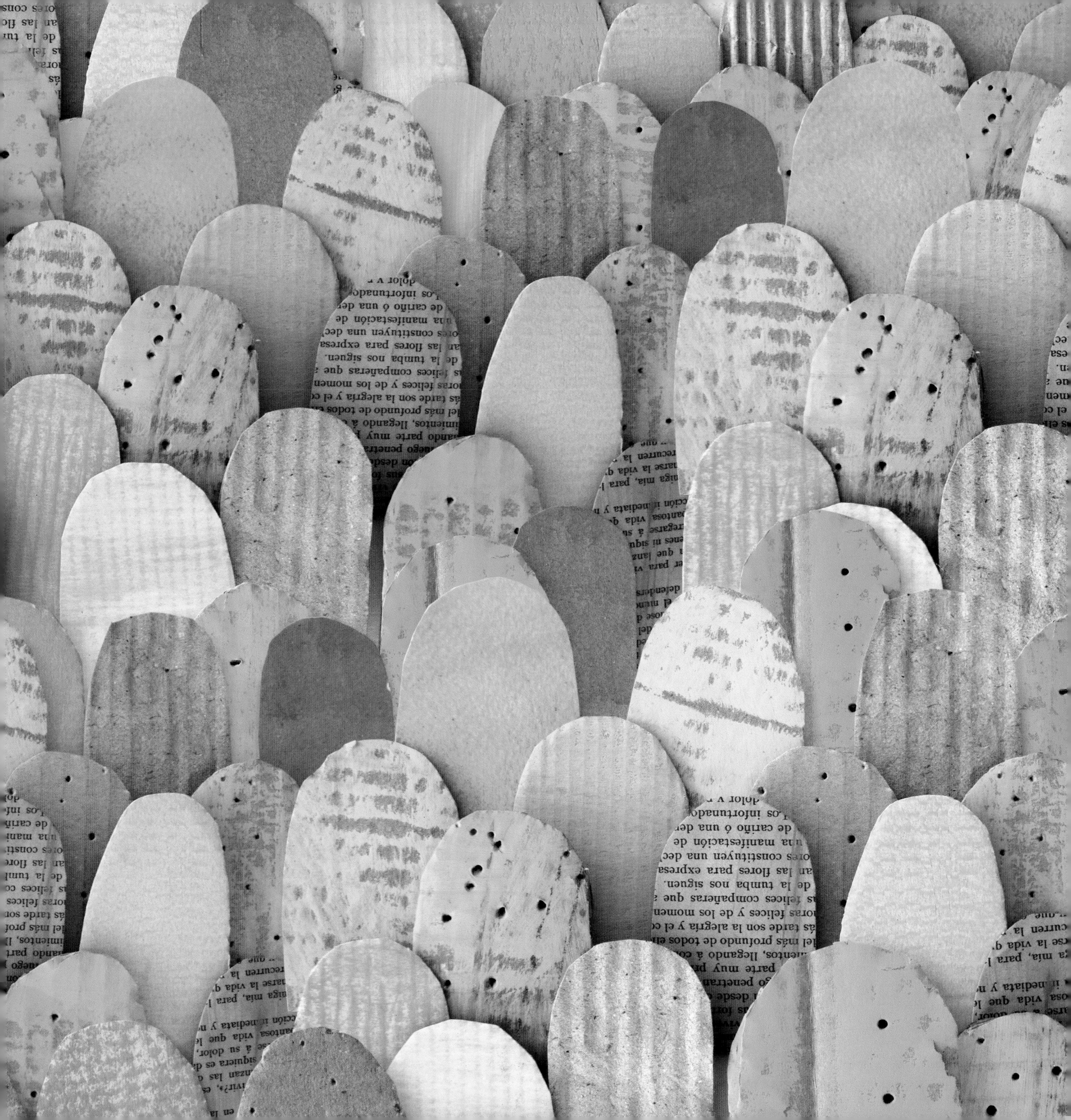

I like the challenges, all the challenges – A. Ll. S

A TEMPLAR BOOK

Published in the UK in 2017 by Templar Publishing,
an imprint of Kings Road Publishing,
part of the Bonnier Publishing Group,
The Plaza, 535 King's Road, London, SW10 0SZ
www.bonnierpublishing.com

First published by Editorial Planeta as *Te quiero (casi siempre)*
Text and illustration © Anna Llenas, 2017
www.annallenas.com
English translation copyright © Templar Publishing, 2017

10 9 8 7 6 5 4 3 2 1

ISBN: 978-1-78370-797-3

English language edition edited by Isobel Boston

Printed in Malaysia

I love you
(nearly always)

t

templar publishing

Roly and Rita

are very

different.

Roly is a
woodlouse . . .

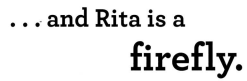
. . . and Rita is a
firefly.

Roly is **strong** and **tough** . . .

. . . **and Rita is** light
and delicate.

Roly is the **king of camouflage . . .**

. . . and Rita is the
brightest
light in the sky.

He is **sensible** and
down-to-earth . . .

. . . while she likes to **daydream**

and lets her imagination **soar.**

Roly likes to be
in control . . .

. . . and Rita likes to
improvise.

Roly thinks Rita is
honest
and **funny** . . .

. . . and Rita thinks Roly
is **independent**
and **mysterious.**

Roly and Rita are very different,
and this is why they like each other.

But then, one day . . .

Rita notices that
Roly's **tough** suit
is far too **hard** . . .

. . . and Roly finds Rita's
light far too **bright.**

Roly thinks Rita
flies **too fast.**

And Rita can't **stand** the way
Roly has to **control** everything.

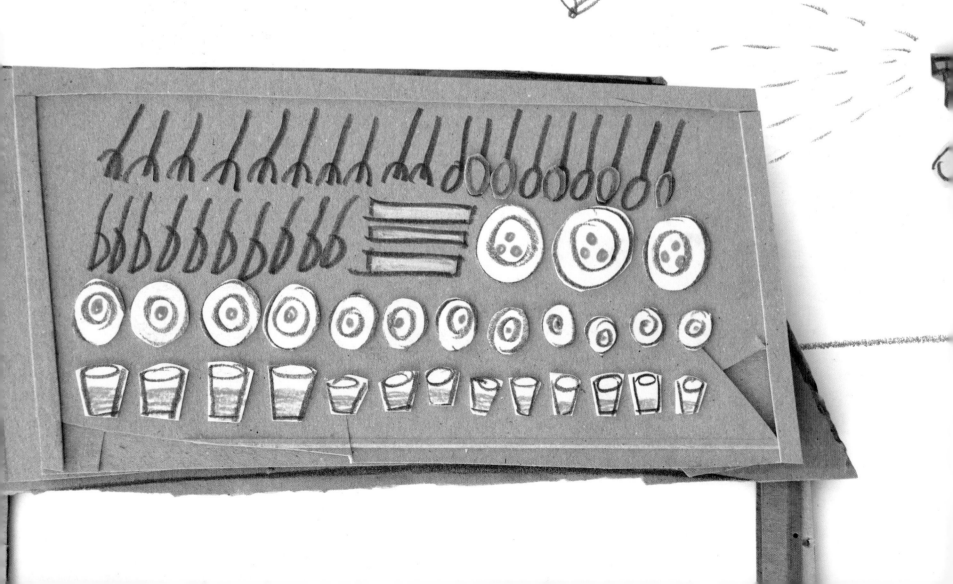

Roly wonders if Rita

is sometimes

too **honest** . . .

. . . and Rita thinks

Roly spends too much

time **alone.**

Roly doesn't like it when Rita
makes a **mess** . . .

. . . and Rita gets
frustrated
when Roly is quiet
and **hides away.**

Roly and Rita know they are
very different . . .

. . . and this makes
them sad.

So **Roly** tries

to soften his **suit**

a little for Rita . . .

... and **Rita** tries to let Roly have the **spotlight** too.

Roly even **trusts** Rita and lets
himself enjoy the ride.
(Well . . . sometimes.)

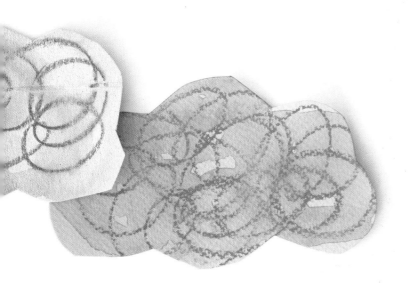

Rita **flies**
a little more
slowly for Roly.

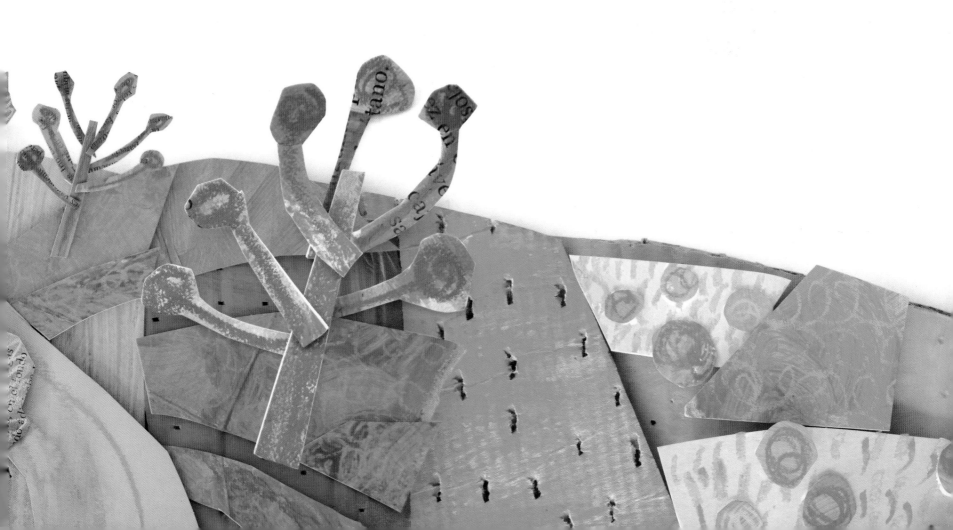

And she gives him space to be
independent . . .

. . . and

mysterious.

Roly gives Rita time to be **creative**, and he always likes to see what she has made.

Roly and Rita know
they are very different . . .

. . . and this is why

they **love** each other.

y destrez
existen otros
aunque ellas mism
n hacer algo más que
confirma mi creencia
misiva me habla de su i
se por unos días con su d
las fuerzas necesarias

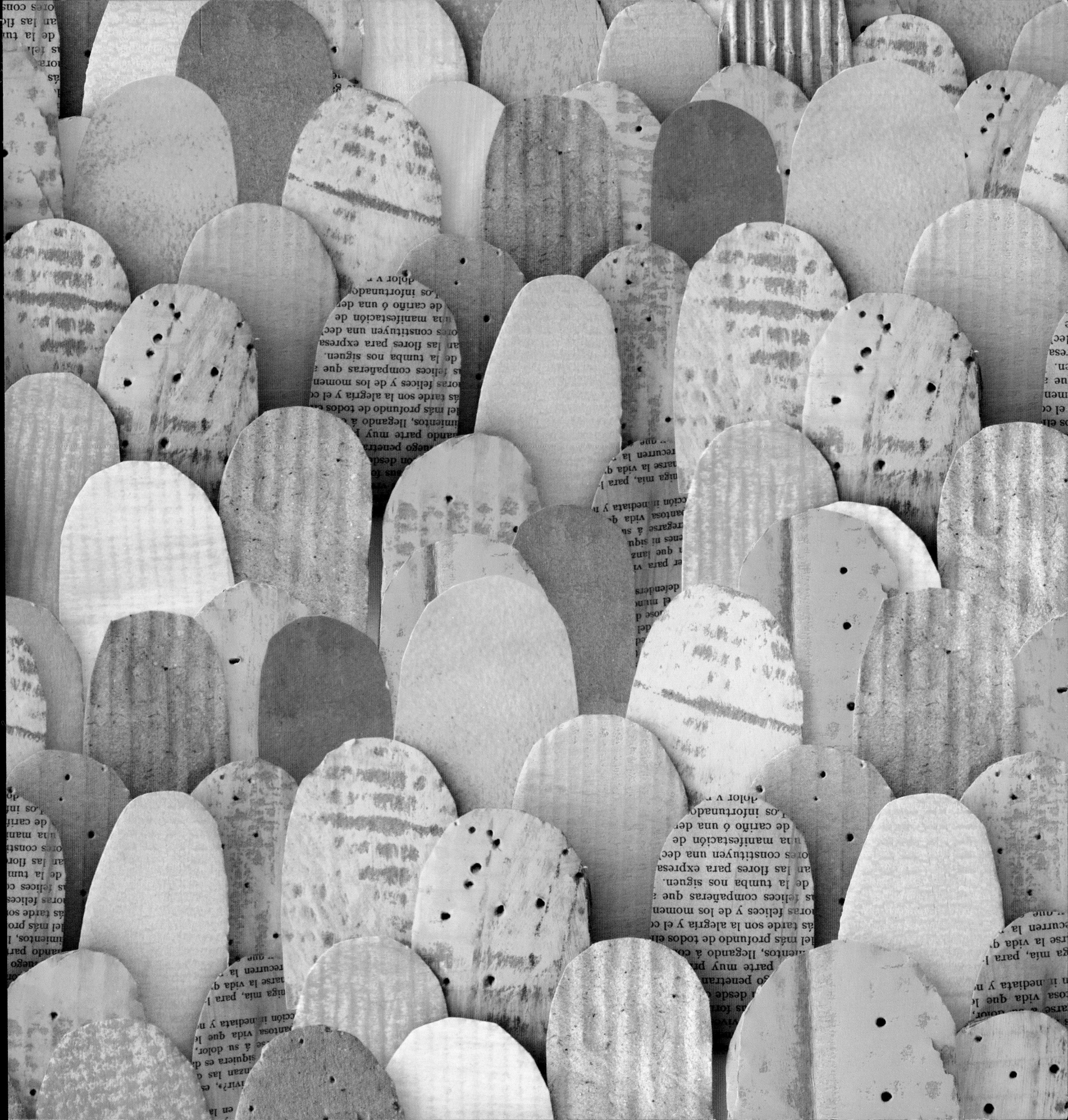

Also by Anna Llenas:

I Love You (Nearly Always) pop-up
ISBN: 978-1-78370-761-4

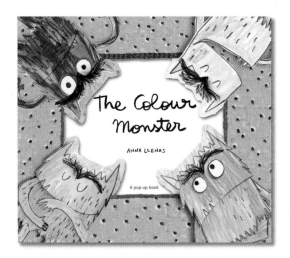

The Colour Monster: a pop-up book
ISBN: 978-1-78370-356-2

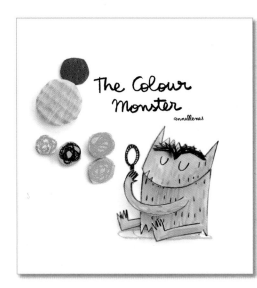

The Colour Monster picture book
ISBN: 978-1-78370-494-1 (Hardback)
ISBN: 978-1-78370-423-1 (Paperback)

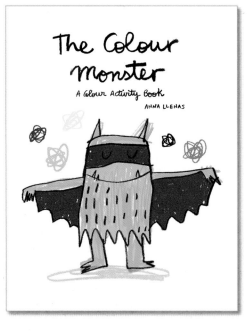

The Colour Monster: a colour activity book
ISBN: 978-1-78370-356-2